AF451002

WHERE DO WE LEARN TO LOVE?

Where do we learn to love?
Amanda Oliveira-Telò
amandatelo.com
© Amanda Telò, 2023
© ALOT, 2023
This book was edited by Amanda Oliveira-Telò (ALOT) in March 2023.
All rights reserved. No part of this publication may be reproduced, stored in a retrieval system, or transmitted in any form or by any means, electronic, mechanical, photocopying, recording, or otherwise, without the publisher's prior permission.

WHERE DO WE LEARN TO LOVE?

Amanda Oliveira-Telò
#SHORTSTORIES #PHOTOS

*To the version of myself who believed she could never...
Thankfully, you were mistaken.*

#Table of contents

"One does not find peace by avoiding life."

- Virginia Woolf

#Introduction

When I love too much, I write. I write to be able to open my chest and take a breath. And breathe again... And survive... Live? For one more day until it all starts again.

Walking in circles trying to understand how to love, overcome, live, and re-enchant myself, if there is an answer. I may write to recharge because living in this world requires more energy than I have to deal with...

Maybe I write to kill something in me, or to suffocate everything that comes out of the box of what was supposed to be me, or what I wanted it to be, everything that overflows and floods. Suffocate in notebooks that I don't dare to reread or even the ability to understand my own handwriting.

It's like a recipe: feel a whirlwind, write until my hand hurts, close the notebook and go live in this world...

Where did the evolution they promised us go? I write because if I didn't, maybe I'd go screaming in the streets or engaging in discussions that I would never win...

So I write about everything that touches, pierces, and crushes me. Everything I'm tired of repeating to my friends, everything I'm uncertain about, everything that angers or enchants me, everything that seems too much to be spoken aloud. *Everything that seems like the world doesn't give room to exist.* I write my story, others' stories, what I wish it was or what it could have been.

I write, close the notebook, and nothing ever changes. How could it?

But maybe I write to dream, and then I dream of everything that the world could be if everyone decided to open their notebooks, throw away what's normal and speak out loud everything that bothers those who created the rules. *What would the world be like if everyone dared to express themselves, to talk about their pains and loves? Truly everyone.*

But as ironic as it may be, I still don't know how to be different or find the courage to break the notebook lock and read everything out loud. But I understand that I need to. Because if everyone thinks like this and stays silent, how do we grow and get out of this? So I write, maybe to breathe, understand, live, or kill. But today, to be free.

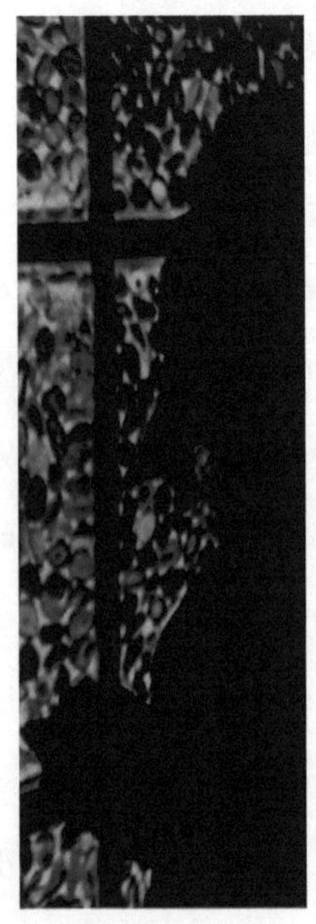

#1 Being

She questioned daily whether life wouldn't be better if she were different. If she could feel differently, act differently. Perhaps without such a strong desire to speak, she could stay silent, let chance decide, or just follow the manual everyone receives from society.

Her constant restlessness had always been a reminder of the emptiness that never fills. So one day, she decided to go for a walk pretending to be someone else.

She slammed the door as she left and walked, relieved, and that relief began to grow, and, with such lightness, she started to float. It was as if all the weight of her body had evaporated until there was no mass left to hold her to the earth.

She floated for days, weeks, until her sense

of time and space was lost, along with everything she once recognised as hers. And it was no longer pretence; she was no longer herself, but she wasn't someone else either.

As she floated through existence without an identity or a place to belong, and for a time that couldn't be calculated, *she existed without living,* unable to remember if it was still possible to return.

#2 Life as it is

Swipe left, swipe right, swipe left...

The dating app stays open for hours, and no one exciting appears.

I receive a Super Like.

Tanned skin, rosy lips almost forming a heart, *nothing extraordinary, but it's a Super Like.* So I look again and reply to the message that almost instantly appears after the match. We chat about being the kings of common names, and then I give him my phone number, and we talk...

Our conversations begin with travel, but they flow endlessly into the realm of all things imaginable and beyond.

John seems like a shelter amid a storm in just a few days of conversation. Weeks pass, and we continue to grow together, discussing deep topics we've never talked about with anyone else.

With each passing day, I become more attached to him, and finally, after weeks, it's time for us to meet in person. FINALLY. *Because, yes, nothing is perfect; he lives 62 miles away.*

But he came all this way for me, and today is the day. He calls to say he's almost here, so I go downstairs to the lobby and wait. When I saw him coming, *average,* I expected butterflies as soon as I saw him. However, I soon censor myself; it's normal to feel strange when meeting someone in person you've only talked to through messages and video, so I don't dwell on it and go with an open heart to meet him.

"Hi, I parked on the other street; I hope it's safe around here," he says with a friendly face. "Hi, yes, it's quite peaceful, but wow, I can't believe you're here," I reply with a slightly higher pitch, hoping he doesn't notice. "Neither can I, but yes, finally," he whispers, hugs me, and the kiss happens instantly, and it's good.

After a short time, the strangeness fades, the conversation flows for hours, and we're already past lunchtime. I want to spend more time with him, talking, connecting, touching his soft, curly hair, kissing his lips, and looking into his brown eyes.

But it's time to go; I've planned a whole itinerary to show him my city, and I almost jump for joy when he holds my hand as we walk.

The good feeling I had through messages translates and intensifies in person; *how lucky I am*; I want all of this to last forever; life like this is worth living.

I show him my favourite places, cinemas, and cafes and tell him things I never thought were relevant to mention, but everything seems interesting to him; he finds me interesting, and *I am interesting to the most interesting person I know.*

I could listen to him talk about films, series, music, and life ideas for hours; every word that comes out of his mouth makes the world better.

We go to the market to buy some drinks; *it's a day to celebrate*; after all, he's here. Back home, I turn on only a warm light and put on a sexy playlist I've never used before; today, I want to make him want to come back *because, my God, how I want to live this again.*

Sparkling wine in glass cups, intense kisses, when he touches me, I feel my body go into a trance, and for the first time, everything seems like it will be alright. Do you know when you think you'll never find someone who makes you feel good in the fullness of a relationship? When he touches me, everything seems possible again.

And he touches me more and more, removing my clothes piece by piece until our bodies meet and connect.

Hours pass quickly, and I fall asleep, feeling like I'm in heaven. But it's time to say goodbye, and *I can only think about our next dat*e. He kept my favourite book, and I kept his. I can hardly wait to hear everything he has to say.

The face-to-face moment is over, but the heart remains warm. The flow of conversation increases, and the longing grows with it. As days go by, we plan a date for next month. We exchange playlists with our favourite songs, talk about movies, and swap digital books.

Today, I insist on seeing him through a video call; I miss his smile. The phone rings, and he answers with a look that mixes love and pain. Something inside me knows that something is coming, and my brain races in anticipation, thinking about everything that could go wrong because of the situation:

1. We live in different cities.

2. We need the financial means to make this trip frequently.

3. In any case, he can't spend several weekends away from home for personal reasons.

My fears become certainties when he starts talking more about the problems than about love. At first, I agree *it would indeed be difficult*, but the conversation continues, and I cry when he says:

And I don't know what to think anymore. He continues to talk and list problem after problem. I try to come up with ideas to solve them, but he promptly adds more problems.

The call ends, and days go by. Whenever I ask to see him on a video call, he tells me it will only make things more difficult. *It's over for him, I know, but he says he wants to take things slower.* When you forcefully brake on a speeding car, you brace for an accident on the

Motorway.

But to me, he's one of those things you don't have the option to give up on easily; I see our potential and the beautiful things we can experience together.

He keeps making everything more complicated, distancing himself, and all my arguments for him to stay seem weak compared to his reasons to leave. But, *my God, I want to show him how committed I am, how much I want him like I've never wanted anyone before.*

I always think about him, wanting to share every tiny event of my life, but now I barely get a response. The sabotage he's doing to our relationship almost drains all my strength. I don't know if I can try anymore; I don't see other people, I don't want to do anything new, and everything is grey again.

I want him, but I can't have him anymore. He talks to me, but he's not here anymore. My only contact with him is through his friends, who, in the meantime, have become mine, especially Anne.

Anne is the girlfriend of John's best friend, Peter. Anne and I have a million things in common besides the fact that we both love best friends. She adds me on social media, and we strike up a conversation. We talked for days, and now that everything is lost with him, in an impulsive move, I decided to spend the weekend with her in her city.

I've always been impulsive, but love gives me an extra boost. I genuinely want to go see Anne in person; I need a change of scenery, but the idea of perhaps bumping into John makes me start looking for tickets to go as early as next weekend.

This whole drama began on Friday, the 10th of March, *exactly two months ago*, and today I'm finally in his city. I send him a message, but he says he's going away and can't see me; my heart tightens, *I'll be here until Sunday, and he won't even try to catch me briefly*. On top of that, John finishes the message by stating that it's not because he's afraid of going back on his decision that he won't try because that possibility doesn't exist; he really doesn't want to see me. *Cold.*

I can try to say that I'm fine, but I'm not; I feel anger, so much anger, because, after everything, this

Where do we learn to love?

isn't how I want things to end.

But talking to Anne always helps; as much as the motivation for being here is based on seeing him, and now he's gone, I need to cling to the rest and at least try to distract myself.

She invites me to go out for drinks with some friends. I open and close all my social media, hoping he'll change his mind and send me a *"Where are you? let's meet up."* But he doesn't, and we almost can't return home; I use my phone until the battery runs out and order a taxi with only 2% left.

But everything works out, and we make it to Peter's house, where we decide to spend the night closer to the city centre for tomorrow's outing. I use the opportunity of Peter's presence to talk about John even more, and we discuss him for hours until I finally fall asleep.

Day breaks and the conversation continues, but today we're shopping, eating, and strolling at the mall. Hours pass until, finally, the awaited notification appears: a message from John, some photos from his trip, and in response, I promptly send pictures of our enjoyable moments at the shopping centre. *But he leaves me confused*; with every message from him, I feel like he might still like me and might want to see me tomorrow, but he still says no.

The day goes by, and Anne, Peter, and I decide to go out for some drinks and dance; tonight, I'll dance, drink a lot, and forget this confusing situation I'm living in. But I can't help but constantly think that the four of us would make a great group of friends.

The club hardly has any queue, but Anne stays to save our spot to ensure we get in first while Peter and I buy some pills to prevent tomorrow's hangover. The pharmacy is far, and the walk is long, but the good thing is we can talk *about John*.

I clarify many things about what John thought of me, and more and more I feel like an idiot for suffering for a man who really doesn't care about my feelings. A man who chooses daily not to love me, not even to try, and who is already fed up with me, has lost interest. I'm sad, but in a way, I always knew everything, *and he's already told me.*

We return and enter the club; it's time to drink; it's an open bar until one in the morning, and we have exactly two hours to drink until we lose our senses. I ask Peter to hold my phone and dive headfirst into the fun. *I forget, but I remember.* One moment I'm happy, thinking everything will work out, and the next, I think of everything that has already gone wrong; he's not here, and I drink another glass.

Electronic music plays, and my consciousness is so low that if country music were playing, I'd be dancing the same way; the music doesn't matter. I drink more and dance, dance with Anne, dance with Peter, drink more.

In the last minutes of the open bar, I notice Peter looking at me differently. Still, I must be crazy or very needy, so I ignore it. But the touches start, the looks intensify, and when I look at Anne, she looks at me just as tempting. My mind races, and I wonder, *"Do they really want this? This could ruin everything, but on the other hand, I have the right to live; I am free."* But I resist, keep dancing, drink more, feel sick only to bounce back to feeling great, and continue drinking. And I kiss more people, drink more, and when I notice, I'm kissing Peter. And Anne. *Both,* one at a time, both at the same time.

And we keep dancing until someone suggests going somewhere quieter, and I hesitate for a moment but think, *"We've come this far; why not?"* And we go.

The alcohol is high, I need to pee, and the street will do; we get in the wrong taxi, then the right one, and head to the motel.

For the first time since the beginning of the night out, I check my phone for messages, a message from John saying nothing important, which I desperately want to respond to, send a *"miss you"* or *"it's so much fun here."* But Anne and Peter don't think it's a good idea, so I don't send it. I put the phone away and returned to living in the moment.

We arrive, and the motel justifies the high price. With a hot tub, and a large round double bed, the perfect setting for a memorable night. *But I'm so drunk that I only remember flashes.*

Foam bath and lots of kisses, sex, moaning, the tub overflows and floods the entire room, we climax, there's nothing left to do, we eat chocolate and sleep.

The hangover is intense, but it's time to head to Anne's house. I order a taxi, and even after taking pills, my head still hurts, and the morning passes, and it's already lunchtime. We talk about how crazy everything was, have no regrets, and life goes on.

We went to the park and met more of their friends and even after all this, the feeling that I want to be with John and be part of all this still lingers, even though I'm unsure how he would react to the information about my night with his friends.

But he clarified that he no longer loved me and lost the passion and desire. *But if he wants to, I still want to and would give anything to know if he still thinks about me as much as I think about him.*

So, when Peter tells me that John wants to see if I'm still in town, I find myself confuse. Is he asking to avoid me or to meet up? And the day runs out without us meeting.

Back home, I woke up to his message asking how everything had been. Still determined to get over him, I said as little as possible. But it's incredible how he needs to give me a little attention, and I throw myself back into the situation. Here I am, telling him everything, or almost everything. I tell him the relevant things, but I don't mention the final part of Saturday night directly, not out of fear but because I don't understand if talking about such personal things with him still makes sense. We were nothing anymore.

I talked to Peter early on Tuesday morning, and he told me he would meet with John. We conclude that if they get to the subject of the night out *(and especially the after-party)*, he will tell everything; after all, there is no reason to hide the events.

But my anxiety increases as this unfolds, and I want to distract myself. But I cannot stop thinking about John and finally start reading the book we exchanged on our first date. I read and connected with the story, and I decided to send him a picture on one of the pages. He replies:

"It is better to leave the book with Anne.

I do not want to see you anymore."

And with that message, I know Peter has told him about Saturday. Honestly, I didn't expect such a reaction; I expected no reaction at all. He made it clear that he doesn't feel anything for me anymore, but this is the end. I felt it before, but now I see, from now on, everything changes, and now he has a reason not to stay. And as much as I try, there's no way back; he doesn't want to listen to me anymore, but that doesn't stop me from trying.

> I really want to talk to you, can you call me? So we can clarify things.

Please, stop talking. Every word I read makes me more nervous.

> Okay, I think what bothers me the most is that it's not fair. You're not being reasonable like you always boasted about being.

If you want to talk to me in 2-3
months, maybe I can speak
rationally.

Maybe I can understand your side.
Maybe I can overlook something.
But not now.

Okay then, I don't want to bother you...
but one thing, I have to give you
something, what should I do?

To be honest, I don't know. Keep it.
Send it through Anne. Throw it away.
Sell it. I don't care.

He doesn't care; he punctuated our relationship with a final mark, no room for commas.

But here I still dream, and I hope that we're having a beautiful and profound conversation about life in some parallel world right now.

But not here, not today, not in this time-space.

Here, we both continue being this, an ending without possibilities, a maybe that will never be.

(*now my heart needs to believe*)

Meanwhile, your gift remains unopened.

#3 Platonic

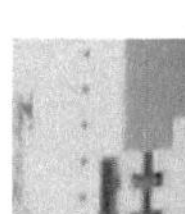

Sitting in the red chair of the doctor's office, I begin to observe a man with short, dark hair who sits in front of me; he seems to lose himself in his thoughts. *Has the day been hard, or is he just trying to remember if he locked his car?* His formal clothes suggest that he might have come straight from work.

I start daydreaming and imagining his life. *He looks like he works in one of those offices where nothing happens all day; he must be bored.* On his fingers, I see no ring nor any sign that there ever was one. His tanned skin tells me that his holidays were spent in the sun, and his well-groomed beard reveals that he cares for himself. The more I observe him, the more intrigued I become; *what is a man like this doing in a doctor's office? What could be his problem?*

A woman opens the door and calls for Alisson, the man in the suit stands up and takes my questions with him. I was called by the doctor at the front door shortly after; my case was just a cold. I leave the office and think about him, then walk to the building's entrance and wait for Alisson; I need to look at him again. When he comes out, I watch him walk out of the car park, seemingly careless.

Curiosity gets the better of me, and I follow him discreetly, not too far away. He stops at the corner pharmacy, buys medicine, walks to the third street parallel to the avenue, and enters it. His steps are quick yet graceful; *who are you, Alisson?*

After four blocks, he stops, takes a key out of his pocket and heads to a building. The eight-story building seems middle-class, and the apartments are not very large; he must live alone.

When he entered, I returned to the doctor's office to get my car, but only to drive to Alisson's place and observe the neighbourhood.

An elderly couple passes by on the street holding

37

hands, the ipê trees leave the street full of flowers, and the sun slowly sets behind a taller building; I turn on the car stereo and wait. *I just wait for him.*

The surprise and excitement come when, after a few hours, he leaves his house in a suit with an Italian cut, walks to the other side of the street where a black car is parked, opens the door and gets in.

When the driver starts the car, I follow closely; we go together to someplace.

It's been three weeks since I started observing Alisson. Now I know that he's a newly graduated lawyer from the city's college, single, 28 years old, works in the morning, attends a master's programme in the afternoon, and goes out every Friday with some friends. An intriguing young man.

Every day I want to know him more; I want to know who he is. I spend my weekends observing his apartment, always waiting for him to come out. I always see him, but he never notices me; *I need him to notice me.*

I'm moving, and now I can see his window on

the sixth floor of my new apartment. I thought my one hundred pounds telescope would be useless, but it served me well; I feel like I'm sitting on his grey sofa in his blue-walled apartment. Every night he sits and watches something, eats, uses his laptop, and talks to someone.

I wish I could see the details up close; I need to get closer, and observing is no longer enough. I want to know what he feels; I want to touch him; *I want him for myself.*

I get up early and go to his office; *it's time to take action.* I spoke to the secretary about a real case, a problem I had with my phone company, and she scheduled me for tomorrow. I barely sleep; I wear my best clothes, fix my hair, and apply gentle perfume and striking lipstick. I practice smiles and expressions in the mirror.

When I finally arrive at the office, I can't contain my excitement; the secretary welcomes me and asks me to wait, but not a minute passes when he opens the door and calls me in. His office is large, bright and filled with books, and he invites me to sit in a centralised set of armchairs. As soon as we sit down, he smiles and gets straight to the point, asking about the case, *but he seems distant*. I explain everything, trying several times to create a personal conversation, but he remains cold and strictly professional.

If he noticed my perfume, he didn't comment; if he found me attractive, he didn't show emotion. I'm right in front of him, but I remain invisible. I leave there and want to forget him; *he's nothing as he seems*.

I return home, and after a few hours, I miss him. When I see him sitting on the sofa, ready to leave, I watch how he constantly checks the time. At that moment, my heart tightens, and I ask myself internally: *what must I do to become the person he's so eagerly waiting for?*

#4
Emotional
(Ir)Responsibility

After many disappointing encounters, she was determined to delete the dating apps and wait for someone interesting to fall from the sky. She was tired of the empty relationships, unfulfilled promises, and brief sexual encounters that didn't lead her to orgasm.

But as a true dreamer, she gave it one more chance. And how could she not? Green eyes, a delightful accent, and great conversation. Moreover, he was new in town, and she couldn't wait to show him everything.

She took him to her favourite cafes, which were closed because it was Sunday. They decided just to walk and walk the entire city for hours. They talked, touched, until finally, the kiss happened, while she thought, *my God, now it seems like it will happen!*

He spoke Italian, voted for the same political parties, and had a smile that lit up the room. He claimed to be quick and intense in things, just like her, so she felt her heartbeat again and wanted to give herself to him. Usually so insecure, she decided to do things differently for him, dive in headfirst and *let whatever God wants to happen (and she hoped He wanted the same as her!).*

Plans were suggested, "how about a movie tomorrow and getting to know the city more during the day?" he asked, "definitely, I don't work in the afternoon, so we can go", she replied, almost shouting with excitement.

"Do you want to go to my place now?" she asked minutes later, "of course", he promptly replied. He promised to make her orgasm, so determined that she believed him. It was close, but for her, it was already enough.

"Stay the night?" she asked as they lay in bed, their bodies sweaty, but he replied, "I can't," put on his clothes and left.

Little did she know that the love that gave her hope that it could work would have such a short lifespan. And it was all too brief.

The next day was a holiday, the sky dawned grey, but her heart shone brightly. She sent a message to check if he was okay and if their plans for the day were still on; he replied, "I just woke up," and after that, nothing, just a suffocating silence for hours. He had new plans for the day, which didn't include her, but she didn't know.

So she couldn't understand why someone would do all that to vanish, why make plans with her, confirm, reserve the whole day, and then not reply anymore, "Why?"

She grew impatient. *Did she do something wrong? Was he really sleeping in late?* She started to become paranoid. He would be online but not view her messages; he would view them but not reply. She tried to reassure herself; *it was okay, he might be busy, something unexpected must have come up, he doesn't like going out in the rain*, but she couldn't help thinking that replying to a message didn't take that much time.

After many attempts, he finally replied, "CALM

DOWN; you didn't do anything wrong. I don't reply on weekdays because I work and study." Now she was officially confused; until yesterday, he was still looking for a job and spent the whole day doing nothing.

But she thought he was too cute to be just another jerk who lied for sex; he seemed too genuine not to be honest. But she wondered, *had he never shown anything, and it was all in her imagination?* Because she wanted it to work so badly, it couldn't go wrong.

So she sent a thousand messages, wanting to understand everything better. *Should she call too?* She didn't think much about it and called, but he didn't answer; at this point, his phone was already on silent.

And she could no longer hold back the tears, knowing that another story without a beginning had ended. Once again, she fell in love with the idea before the person.

"I'm not the right guy for you. Let's not take this any further," were the last words he sent her.

And all she wanted was to sleep and wake up on Sunday, start over and do things differently. Maybe to enjoy the day again or to have the chance to hear in the end, "That was fun; let's do this again someday," or "we'll bump into each other someday, for real."

Because she dreamt of love but had a habit of giving herself to those who didn't give back, of feeling intensely what was lukewarm, of being too much for those who were nothing.

It was intense for her but just an inconvenience for him.

But she knows if there were a time machine, she would return to Sunday's beginning.

#5 Day by day

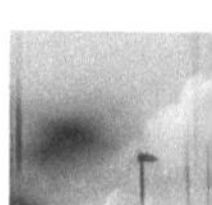

Opening one's eyes and starting a new day. A simple routine, but when performed by mere bones, it becomes a curious spectacle to observe.

How can one open their eyes when there are no eyeballs left? How can one get up when the muscles responsible for movement no longer exist?

Yet, defying everything, she would rise, day after day, not out of desire but simply because her bones had learned to move automatically.

Every day she felt an awakening; before she knew it, she was sitting in front of the computer.

What needs to be done will be done; that had always been her motto. And her bones remembered. Moving every day, even when it went against all the laws of the universe.

One day she had to leave her home and go to the market, and the fear of what others would think upon seeing her walking down the street nearly made her give up on going out.

However, the reality was that, once upon a time, walking skeletons were used to terrify many people. Now, in a world where transformation was daily, she still felt connected to a group.

And so she continued walking, and as she passed by people who still showed skin and muscles, she wondered if it was still possible to return to that state.

But it had been so long since she had been what she was that it seemed impossible to transform into anything else.

#6 Three bottles

Today, I really need a drink.

I'm not usually excited about work socials, but the first one is always interesting. At the first social event, we genuinely see everyone for the first time, outside of all those rules that surround working hours. So, I want to make a good impression; perhaps that way, I can make new friends. *I really need friends.*

"Do you think the black one with the slit up the leg is better or the tighter red one?" I ask my mum, holding up two dresses in front of the camera during the video call.

"Unless you're going to a work social to cheat on your husband, that red one is a bit much," she complains.

"Oh, Mum, I just want to make a good impression," I retort, displeased with her answer.

"That's what I'm saying; the black one is more serious," she concludes.

"Alright, I'll go with the black one" I agree; it's easier to concur with her than to argue. After all, I've already left her alone; I don't need more reasons for her to be angry.

"When you try it on, send me a picture; now, I've got to go; I have a pot on the stove," she says while running with her phone in her hand towards the kitchen.

"No problem, thanks for the help; I love you, bye!" I say, hurrying. I hang up the call and become aware of the silence that fills the room. Every time he travels, the house feels so empty. Even though we have our disagreements, I still want him here... But today, I'll distract myself.

An hour later, I rush down the stairs as fast as my heels allow. I always think I have plenty of time, and in the end, I'm late; I don't know how it happens, but it always happens.

My taxi is already waiting when I open the door. Today, I don't even want to think about walking twenty minutes in these heels on a night that's not warm. What happened to summer?

Last week, I was struggling to sleep because the heat was suffocating me, and today, when I want to show off my legs, the cold appears again. Sometimes living in London annoys me.

B

R

E

A

T

H

E

"Hi, you made it," Lisa says as soon as she sees me enter the bar, "come sit here; there's plenty of room; Simon reserved this whole table for us."

Lisa is my closest colleague at work, and I'm glad

she's already here. Before sitting down, I look around at their chosen impressive bar. There are three huge rooms, all decorated in an industrial style, with lots of artwork on the walls and solid wooden tables.

We're in a room entirely reserved for us, with a table that stretches almost from the beginning to the end of the space, like the communal hall in Harry Potter. To my surprise, there were still many places to sit. I'm still shocked that not all Brits are as punctual as in the movies.

"Hi, yes, everything worked out today, and I'm excited to have a drink with you all," I reply, looking at Lisa and the four other team members whose names I still don't know, "where's Simon?" I ask, missing our boss.

"Oh, he was here, but I think he went to take a call; I don't know how that man does it; he never takes a minute off," says Lisa, chuckling.

"Absolutely, once I got an email at four in the morning on a Saturday; I wonder what his wife thinks of that," I recall; it was indeed a memorable event.

"100% Simon! But he's nice, doesn't pressure us to be like that, so I don't complain," Lisa replies, smiling

HOT & COLD
HOME COOKED
FOOD
at LUNCHTIME
Coca-Cola

and topping up her wine glass, "but enough about him, tell me about you! Is your hubby in town today? Did you leave him at home?"

"Oh, I wish! He went to Paris yesterday and won't be back until Monday," I reply, smiling, but inside I want to cry... or scream… I think that's almost always the answer when someone asks about him. Twice a week, sometimes for four days... And from what he says, the more trips, the better… I don't know how long I can keep answering or living like this. Lisa pulls me out of my thoughts by asking what I'll drink, and I answer:

"Oh, I'm not sure yet; I'll go to the bar to see; want to come with?" I ask, already standing up.

"I'll wait for the guys to decide if they want to order more stuff; if you want to go first, I'll go after," she says.

"Alright, see you soon," I say as I grab my bag and head towards the bar, desperately needing that drink.

At the bar, I order a bottle of Chardonnay just as I spot Simon on the other side of the counter. I wave, and he waves back, picking up his drink and coming my way.

"I'm glad you came!" he exclaims with a smile. I

like his outfit today, I think as I return the compliment. I pay, take my Chardonnay and walk with him back to the table.

The night passes faster than I'd like; I'm having fun. I plan to go out with Lisa next weekend, and I think a good friendship is blossoming. But as the hours go by, one by one, everyone leaves.

"And then there were two!" Simon declares with a playful smile.

Today is one of those days when I'm not excited to return to the empty flat. So, two hours and another finished bottle later, in the middle of a conversation about *The Office*, I find myself paying attention to how he licks his lips lightly every time he stops talking. *Sexy.*

When I started working at this company, I had a slight crush on him. Still, because of our partners, I put up a mental barrier against any indecent thoughts that might occur to me. Or at least I try. We know we can't control our thoughts. But we can control actions.

But now, looking at the dimple on his cheek when he smiles, his intense look on me while I speak, I realise that the dark blue shirt with two buttons undone that he chose for today makes me want to undo the others.

Has he always been this handsome, or have I had too much Chardonnay? As I take off my jacket, trying to cool down, I believe I'm sweating...

"Feeling warm?" he asks as he fills my glass with the rest of the bottle.

I think *you have no idea*, but I only reply:

"Yes, I think I've had too much wine," I answer, grimacing and alternating my look between him and the bottle, "You're making me drink more!"

"We're only finishing the third bottle; I don't do anything you don't want... let me drink this wine then," he retorts, raising his hand to take my glass.

"Hey, hey, hey," I say, taking the glass from his hand as our hands meet in the middle of the table.

And then I shiver... I thought these things only happened in books or movies, but I swear I shivered when our hands touched.

"Husband waiting for you at home?" he asks, ultimately cutting the atmosphere and momentarily pulling me out of my ecstasy. Another question about him, here we go... *And right now*. I can't stand answering this anymore. And I don't want to talk about "husband" now. But I say:

"No, he's travelling... And you, your wife, must be missing you?" I ask; *I would be*, I think, already scolding myself.

"Oh, no, she has her own things, and we're just living like this," he replies with an expression that leaves me confused - is it sadness? Apathy? It certainly doesn't seem like happiness.

"Is everything alright at home?" I ask, even more curious.

"Yes, sorry, I think I've also had a bit too much to drink, I think it's time to go, but I don't want to arrive home like this... Want to go for a walk? I'll walk you home afterwards," he suggests in a very gentle tone.

The invitation surprises me, but I also need to

breathe some fresh air, although walking in the cold in a dress and high heels doesn't seem like the best choice. But alcohol already affects my decisions, and I accept it.

As we leave the bar, I feel a gust of wind hit me, making me shiver and almost regret agreeing to go for this walk.

"Feeling cold now?" he asks.

"A bit, it's a bit colder than I expected; I think I grabbed a jacket that's too thin," I reply, already shivering.

And taking off his jacket and offering it to me, he suggests:

"Use mine; I'm still feeling warm."

I hesitate momentarily, but the cold is intense, so I accept. We walk, searching for a spot with a better view of the Thames. I've never seen this place so calm and quiet. The cold wind enters through the slit in my dress as I wrap myself more in Simon's jacket.

I look to the side, and he's looking at me.

"Are you okay?" I ask with a half-awkward smile as he stares at me with the most tempting look I've ever seen. It seems like he, like me, is struggling to resist.

"Nothing... nothing... How are you feeling?" He asks, quickly changing the subject.

"I think I'm okay, less cold now, and actually," I pause, "more than okay; thank you for the night," I say, sincerely grateful. I needed this night.

And out of nowhere, I feel something I haven't felt in a long time: courage. Sensing the situation, I look at him and say,

"Actually, can I make a confession? I'll probably regret it, and it might change our relationship forever, but you know what?..." I ask, almost regretting bringing up the topic.

He laughs and says,

"You can't say something like that and not finish the story. Come on, miss, I accept the risks and consequences... Go ahead... You can speak." He insists, with a genuinely curious look.

"Okay, you asked for it, don't forget," I whisper, my heart almost jumping out of my chest.

And I began to talk about how much I liked him

at our first meeting and even mentioned to my mother that he was my ideal type, intelligent, friendly, smiling, playful and that our conversation lasted two hours. I slept some nights fantasising about him.

"But I know it's wrong and 100% unrequited. I don't want to act on it. I want to tell you... I don't know why. I think regret is already coming," I babble, panicking about why I decided to say that. I ruined everything on the first day I drank too much.

"I'm sorry, I went too far," I acknowledge immediately.

"Don't be silly. You didn't go beyond any limit. I said I accepted the risks and consequences," he says, in a calmer voice than I expected.

"I know, but saying these things aloud doesn't make sense, making me break out in a cold sweat. I have my husband, and you have Gia, and this may be a fantasy to keep me happy, so sorry for sharing," I speak so fast that I almost lose track of my words.

"Don't be silly; you don't have to apologise. I already said it's okay. I also have a confession," he says gently, stepping towards me. "When I interviewed you, I slept and woke up thinking of you. Of course, there was all the work part, but I don't think I've ever met anyone who smiled like you, and you're so beautiful... I could hardly wait for you to accept the job so I could see you daily. And the flirting, I always thought it was just my imagination, but I admit I always hoped it was true... And I know it's wrong to feel all this. Wrong, but I can't help the excitement I feel when I see you coming."

I can't believe what I'm hearing. Okay, breathe... I think I'm losing it. And all I can say is,

"Yes, totally wrong, but I understand you. Every time I look at you..." I interrupt myself before I say too much, but my expression speaks for me.

He takes another step towards me, touches my face, and whispers,

"I don't think doing it just once will hurt."

"I don't know, I don't know if I could live with the guilt," I confess, taking a deep breath and trying to resist the urge to jump into his arms and give in right then and there, in the cold, with the risk of being seen.

"Look, we've done our best, resisted so far, but... well, I know what I want to experience now, and you?" he says, with a look that alternates between my eyes and my mouth, with an intensity that makes me burn.

My values, morals, principles, plans, everything shrinks in the face of my desire to kiss him right now. This is what I want to experience now.

I breathe and kiss him, embracing every consequence it may bring.

When he kisses me, I feel alive again. I feel desired, looked at, and appreciated; he kisses my neck, runs his hand over my body, and makes me want more and more. I no longer feel the cold, and adrenaline no longer holds me back.

After a few minutes, reality makes me take a step back. *What am I doing?*

"I think it's time to go home now before I do

something stupid," I admit, grabbing my phone and immediately calling a taxi.

"Are you sure? We can go somewhere more private if you prefer," Simon whispers, with a look that shows he doesn't want to let the opportunity pass.

"Yes, we've already done more than we should have," I affirm, sincerely thinking about how I got to this point.

"But I know you want more," Simon insists.

"I can't deny that, but that's why I should go home. Alone," I reply as I struggle to walk to the taxi that has just arrived, the situation make me feel dizzy.

"Bye and sorry for anything," I say as he gives me one last kiss.

"You have nothing to apologise for; take care," he exclaims, waving and smiling as I enter the car.

Five minutes in the taxi pass in a blur as I get lost thinking about what happened tonight. It's not guilt, but an uncomfortable feeling still haunts me.

I arrive at my empty apartment and still can't describe my feelings. Adrenaline races through my heart,

and I can't contain the thoughts that overwhelm me.
What am I doing? I keep asking myself.

So I open the fourth bottle, light a cigarette, and sit
on the sofa, relaxing my body and mind until I realise
where I am is not where I should and *want* to be.

69

#7 I Know, but it passes...

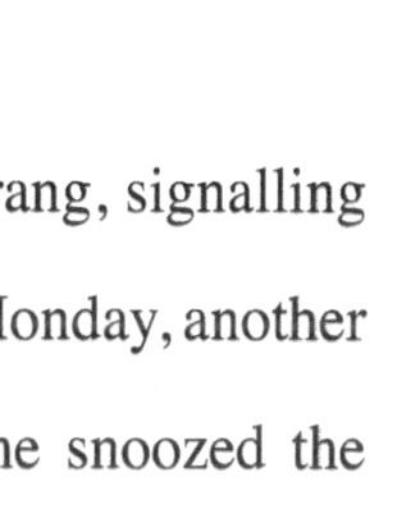

It was 8 am when her alarm clock rang, signalling that it was time to start the day. Another Monday, another week. She couldn't take it anymore. She snoozed the alarm on her phone, but the sleep was already gone. It had become routine so fast. As soon as the alarm went off, anxious thoughts overtook her.

And what did she do to avoid it? She grabbed her phone and began scrolling through the feed for hours until she couldn't afford to stay in bed any longer. But time passed quickly, and she could no longer postpone life.

Dragging herself to the edge of the bed, she slowly put on her socks that had slipped off her feet in the middle of the night, and piece by piece, step by step, she got ready to live.

The morning started slow, and every time she looked at the clock, it seemed like time was moving slower. She worked from home, but that didn't stop her from trying to follow a regular routine, including procrastination for the first hour after turning on the computer.

"I forgot about the tea; now it must be cold," was the first thing she muttered to herself while holding the cold mug. She poured the tea down the sink and put the water to heat once more; it was past time to start working.

Three hours passed as if it were twenty minutes; she hadn't eaten yet, just got up a few times to have more tea and go to the bathroom.

Half of the three hours were used for procrastination, and the other half was spent doing everything much slower than she would like, but it was time for a break.

Anxiety was already intense, and the to-do list was still long, so she decided to escape from it all and watch an episode of *Friends* while smoking a joint with tobacco. She had been smoking every day for two years but didn't like to label herself as addicted. She preferred to say that she wanted to enjoy the phases and moments of life and that the urge would pass soon; at least, that's what she said about everything.

And it was time to work, and the second part of the day, which used to take hours to pass, passed too. At night, she was exhausted and disappointed by the emptiness that was so great that it filled up all the space on the sofa.

So she drank good wine and smoked more until she got sleepy and went to bed, permanently later than she should, to start it all over again.

#8 Monument

Where there was once a void now stood a monument that defied understanding. Its imposing and unexpected presence aroused curiosity and discomfort.

People crowded around it, trying to capture every angle in their photos.

No one knew where it came from or who put it there. The monument occupied two entire blocks, disregarding the streets that were once there, disrupting traffic and all the flow of people.

Videos went viral online; the monument was an enigmatic figure for everyone. Newspapers covered it day and night while scholars tried to understand how something of such magnitude was placed in the middle of the city without anyone noticing. Attempts to remove it were intense, but all failed; it was too heavy.

Weeks passed until what was once so strange and uncomfortable became part of everyday life. The videos no longer received views, and reports lost interest.

Months passed until people who were once startled became accustomed to its imposing presence and began to not imagine the landscape without it.

Years passed until what was once not there became something that always was.

And the population that on the first day pointed their cameras and was astonished now no longer remembered how it all started.

"We get used to things to save our lives.
Which gradually wears out, and from getting so used to
things, we lose ourselves.
We get used to it, I know, but we shouldn't."

- Marina Colasanti

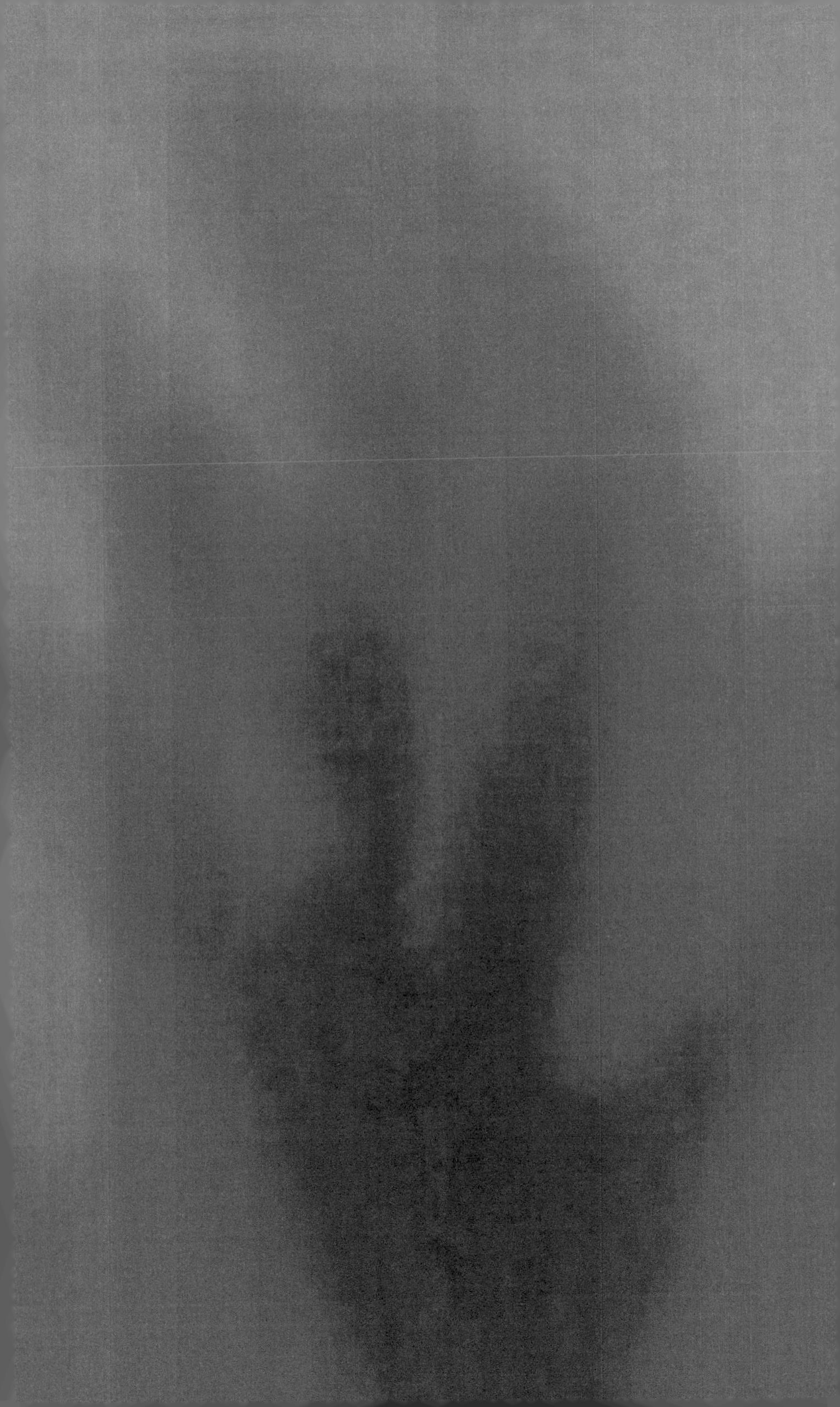

#9 The End

I cry as I press the button and wait for the lift.

It was never my dream to work in a hotel, but today, after saying goodbye to each of those people with whom I shared my routine for over three months, my chest tightens, almost taking away my breath. Anguish, I think that's the name... I always feel anguish when I see something end; it gives me fear, insecurity, and longing. And all of this mixes within me as the elevator goes up to the eighth floor.

The lift has never seemed so slow.

I unlock the door and hear the sound of the TV on; I avoid the living room, go straight to the bathroom, and close the door. Today I don't want to deal with anything else, but two knocks on the door interrupted my plans.

"What are you doing in there?" he says impatiently, irritated again.

"Nothing, I'm just using the bathroom; I'll be out soon - I breathe - I just need a few more minutes," I say, trying not to get stressed, not today.

I don't want to tell him I'm sad again that another job didn't work out.

"Always a problem with you; hurry up, we need to talk," he shouts.

I wash my face and breathe; opening the door and talking is better than starting a discussion today. Not today. I head towards the living room, where I find him sitting on the sofa.

"I've packed my things, and I'm leaving tomorrow," he says without reluctance, with the naturalness of someone saying they're going to the store to buy milk.

"What? Leaving for where?" I ask, trying to understand everything.

"I said I had something to tell you, so I'm telling you, I'm moving to São Paulo, and then I'll send you the details of how we deal with the rest of the things," he responds impatiently.

São Paulo? What is he talking about? What rest of

the things?

"What? Why? What are you talking about?" I shout; nothing makes sense; I need more information. It can't be what it seems. Not now, not after everything I did to make this relationship work. Of everything I accepted. Of everything, I gave up. He can't just leave without a conversation. And to speak like that, as if it's nothing?

I remain silent momentarily, trying to understand everything he said, but nothing makes sense.

"Answer me; I don't understand. Are you leaving me?" I ask, already crying.

"Leaving you? Oh, come on! Leaving you would put you out on the street with no money, but I'm leaving. I've already paid for 3 months' rent; I know you'll survive," he refutes without further explanation.

"If you're leaving this marriage, us, everything we fought to build... no, that can't be it" I say, unable to contain the tears streaming down my face.

"That's exactly it; I'm glad you understand. I want to finalise this without drama, without unnecessary conversations, that's why I've already packed my bags, and my decision is final," he responds in a cold voice tone.

"You said, 'After all we've fought for,' I'm tired of fighting. Everything is so difficult with you. You're never happy, always crying. Sometimes I don't even want to come home to avoid dealing with your unhappiness," he yells in a tone that now sounds like a stranger talking; my husband would never speak to me like that.

"Why are you being so cruel? Did you drink? Are you okay? It's better if we take a break today and talk tomorrow with a clear head," I plead, desperate to make this situation pass.

"No, I'm soberer than ever, just tired," he rebuts, lying about his sobriety.

"I'm tired too, but I keep fighting for us," I say, almost yelling again.

"For us or for the ideal relationship you have in your head?" he vociferates with the coldest expression I've ever seen.

And I become confused, and anger wells up inside of me.

"I've always fought for us, for what we planned and dreamed of together; I gave up my life for you, I gave up my job for you, I started again for your dreams... And of course, I cry; it isn't easy, but I'm still here trying every day for us, for the future we want to create together... How dare you say that?" I scream, no longer able to control my tone of voice.

"It's the truth; you try, but it doesn't work; I need someone who brings me happiness, not someone who just knows how to demand from me," he coldly rebuts.

"I can't believe you said that, I only demand the minimum, attention, love, and presence, but if you think that way, you're right. It's been over for a long time, and I've spent a lot of energy trying to hold this relationship alone," I confess, already tired but not believing that this is happening.

"Great, then we agree. I'm leaving today," he says, standing up from the sofa and heading towards the bedroom.

But I no longer have the strength to go after him. This is the end, and my greatest fear has become a reality.

And it was he who made the final decision.

I lose track of time, but when I see him, he leaves the room with two suitcases and a backpack and says:

"When you're calmer, we'll talk about the rest, divorce and paperwork," he asserts, emotionless.

"Are you leaving like this? Are you sure?" I ask, with smudged makeup running down my face and a glimmer of hope.

"I'm sure," he opens the door, leaves the key on the table next to it and whispers, "And if I knew it would end like this, I wouldn't have started."

I can't believe this is the last thing he says before slamming the apartment door. Wow. After seven years, this is the end.

As the sound of his footsteps becomes distant in the long hallway, I revisit my memories in search of the moment when everything started to crumble.

As much as it hurts, this is where I need to be to see and finally understand.

And if I knew it would end like this, I would do it all over again.

Where do we learn to love?

"Everything that lives, lives because it changes; it changes because it passes; and because it passes, it dies. Everything that lives perpetually becomes something else, constantly negates itself, avoids life."

- Fernando Pessoa

#10 Journey to Within

She loved to have peace, but unfortunately, she never learned how to turn off her thoughts and find the silence within herself. However, every morning, she would wake up and keep everything around her turned off for the first few hours of the day.

It was the least she could do because even without wanting to, her brain followed the same daily script of simulating dialogues that never existed, remembered problems she didn't want to solve, and felt guilty for being late even though she had no set time or place to go.

But one day, she read a snippet of an article on the internet that said how people thought differently; not everyone had voices in their head, or internal dialogues and monologues, some contemplated the silence, and she was fascinated. If there were different people, perhaps she could also be different and have peace.

She decided to find a way to journey within herself and make it happen, no matter what it took. Finding a solution was long, but she created her formula by gathering information from various sources. She was ready to go.

The surprise came when she found a forest inside her head. Up close, the whirlwind of noise that disrupted her peace was the singing of birds, the river's rushing, laughter, the wind in the leaves, and the voices of the people she loved.

But it was all everywhere, a bed in the water, a house in pieces, a person walking through the mountains, and many thoughts with nowhere to be. So she decided to organise the forest that was herself.

She started by organising all the scattered memories in files separated by dates. She spent days in this process because she couldn't resist revisiting each one.

She organised a party, set up a small camp, invited all the lost people, and spent days there because she had so much to talk to each one.

After rebuilding the house and putting all the furniture back, she spent several days organising everything. She had collected so much cool memorabilia to decorate with.

She built a bench on top of a small mountain with a view of the entire forest and placed a sign next to it that said "inspiration corner" because it was.

It took her over seven days, but when she finally finished, she sat on the river's edge and put her feet in the water. And she understood. The only path to peace was to listen to the sounds of thoughts and embrace.

#11 To Remember

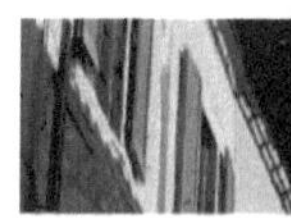

She woke up to her phone ringing. *Was it really ringing or the alarm?* The bitter taste in her mouth set the tone for the confusion swirling in her head: *Am I late? Where am I? What time is it? What was that noise?* She searched for her phone in the empty and cold bed sheets, to no avail.

She opened her mouth and took a deep breath, *this phone had to be here somewhere,* and she decided to get up and search for it. In the end, she found it inside the pillowcase, with a call from an unknown number, but she never answered those. *I'm not late, I'm in Italy, alone in this apartment, eight o'clock at night, too early to sleep, too late to do something, but I'm hungry.* So she decided to open the window to breathe in some fresh air.

From up there, she saw someone waving.

"Hi, good to see you; I have a package for you

that arrived at my apartment," said the neighbour whose name she couldn't remember.

"Ah, yes, are you coming up? I'll come down to your apartment in a bit if that's okay," she asked, now more awake.

"Yes, I'll wait for you," the neighbour affirmed, smiling and entering the building.

She decided to brush her teeth, change clothes, and go out to eat something. She had cried all day because living the dream was not always happy. Sometimes the emptiness returned, her chest ached, and she cried for hours until she fell asleep, already drained of energy. But despite not being excited and her face a little puffy, spending another night without putting her feet outside the apartment didn't seem like a good idea.

She picked up her package and invited her neighbour to dinner, who hadn't eaten yet, and agreed even though he was surprised by the invitation. She didn't mind eating alone, but on nights like this, she knew exactly what she needed, and it was too late to message anyone else.

Although she had never really talked to the

neighbour, he always seemed friendly. Still, from what she heard, his life differed significantly from hers.

Even so, she was happy, despite the initial discomfort, to talk to someone who saw the world a little differently. Perhaps a new perspective on life was all she needed.

At the restaurant, they talked about the reasons that brought them there. He, a man in his thirties taking a break from his finance job, and she, a woman in her forties seeking inspiration for a new book (*or a new life*). The two met midway through the journey, and she was grateful for the stranger who kept her company.

Her thoughts were interrupted by the carbonara served with plenty of cheese on top, accompanied by garlic bread and bruschetta. *I will definitely come back here.*

Before eating, she took a sip of the white wine she didn't know the name of and thought of *adding* wine-tasting classes to her to-do list. And after two minutes of eating, she was sure she would never forget those flavours. *Is food always this good, or am I just famished?*

And she indulged herself more.

She also indulged at the moment. They chose a table outside the restaurant, with a view of the street, which at this time of night was more crowded with tourists than ever. The accordion played "Bella Ciao," while some people took pictures. Every person who passed by spoke a different language, laughed differently, and wore different clothes. Being in a place like this made her remember the vastness of the world and its possibilities.

She took a bite of garlic bread and started to appreciate the old buildings around her, with their pastel colours that looked like the landscape paintings every grandmother had at home. She felt like she was under the Tuscan sun, even at night.

After taking a sip of wine, the conversation reached another level. Talking about family always caused a lump in her throat and a sense of longing. However, that stranger understood her. Despite their differences, they connected and embraced each other.

At that moment, while drinking wine, dining in good company, amidst accents, in a place that seemed like a movie set, the pain she felt in her chest earlier seemed like a thing of the past. *It always passes*, she remembered.

She also remembered how much she loved life and why she still tried, despite everything. Sometimes, it was hard to forget. She felt it every time she overcame fear and opened up to life, every time she dared to be present and to be.

*"Life shrinks or expands
in proportion to one's
courage."*

- Anais Nin

Where do we learn to love?

#Acknowledgments

I still can't believe I'm here. Doing this. Writing a book... The first, the hardest, is when we test the process and ourselves and learn to overcome fear, shame, and insecurity. Writing a book always seemed like a distant dream to me, but as it became a reality, it made me think about everything we could do.

So I would like to thank my family first, who, even when my choices didn't make much sense, have always been and are by my side, giving love and support.

Mom, you taught me what it means to love even in our differences and be strong and resilient, and of course, you helped me cross Colombo and reach the other side of the world. Thank you for everything you have done and are; I admire and love you.

Bebê (Marina for those less familiar), I honestly don't know what I would do without you; you are my light, my peace, the person who reminds me how good people can be and all we can do. Who teaches me daily that dreaming is worth it and sometimes realising it is simpler than we think.

Vó Marina, I wish you were here; I still miss you daily. Thank you for showing me what unconditional love is in various ways and moments.

Robbie, my life and adventure partner, thank you for letting me into your life and venturing into it with you. Thank you for all the times you welcomed and loved me, even when I couldn't do that for myself.

Dad, thanks for staying and keeping up, even when most choose to go.

I would also like to thank my friends, each one of who taught me what friendship means. Thank you for sharing stories, moments, cigarettes, and glasses of wine with me. Life is so much better with you by my side.

I would also like to thank the teacher who encouraged me to love literature even more, teacher Juliana Alves from Gastão Vidigal School in Maringá; thank you for sharing your passion; the smell of vanilla still reminds me of the good feeling of being in your literature classes.

A special thank you to Beatriz Suzuki, an incredible psychologist; you guided me and helped me see things I didn't know existed and reminded me that despite all the changes, I still remain. Now I no longer have to run away to get where I want; I can finally walk and enjoy the view.

Thanks also to the girls from the writing club, especially Joyce Bandeira, who awakened me from my long sleep when I had forgotten why we write. Many of the texts here came from the fantastic writing club @ somosvalentinas. Thank you for being an inspiration, support, and comfort.

Many of the texts here came from the fantastic writing club @somosvalentinas. Thank you for being an inspiration, support, and comfort.

I would also like to thank Hada Maller, author of the book "The Island of Lost Feelings." Having someone so close who writes and is incredibly inspiring motivated me to try to do the same.

I also want to thank everyone who read my stories, helped me review, and gave me feedback, which made this book possible. In particular, I want to thank my sister, Marina, who is always incredible, and Bia Nunes, who deserves a special thank you for embarking on all my crazy projects; thank you for being a friend who is also a soul sister. I also thank Isa and Mari, who read this book before everyone else and gave me valuable feedback and the motivation I needed to publish; finally, you are amazing! And Lari, who, even before I thought about writing a book, always encouraged me to keep writing on my blog; friend, you are light.

Finally, thank all those who inspired and supported me on this journey, helping me to move forward and believe in myself.

Thank you to each and every one of you and to everyone who has crossed my path in life, including the inspirations for some of my stories. Thank you for showing me what love is (*and what it definitely is not!*).

Thank you for the warmth, respect, affection, truth, connection and love.

With you, I have learned to love.

Thank you. I love you all.

Where do we learn to love?

amandatelo.com

#About Amanda Oliveira-Telò

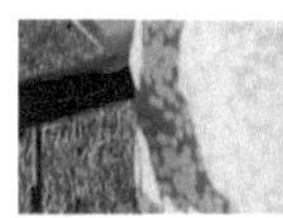

Amanda Oliveira-Telò is a passionate writer and creator from Maringá, Brazil. Her journey led her to Liverpool where she currently resides as a social media specialist , designer and creator of templates, notebook *(and now, books)*.

Driven by a constant yearning for answers, Amanda found solace in writing, exploring the intricacies of life, love, and the pursuit of authenticity.

Her debut book, "Where Do We Learn to Love?", captures these reflections, a testament to her unwavering courage and relentless quest for truth. Writing a book was once an elusive dream, but Amanda nurtured it with determination.

With each story, she unravels the complexities of self-love, connections with others, and the essence of existence. In this captivating collection, she immortalises moments of courage, love, and the profound beauty of the human experience.